Norman the Norman from Normandy

Philip Ardagh

Norman the Norman from Normandy

Illustrated by
Tom Morgan-Jones

Barrington  Stoke

First published in 2020 in Great Britain by
Barrington Stoke Ltd
18 Walker Street, Edinburgh, EH3 7LP

www.barringtonstoke.co.uk

Text © 2017, 2018, 2020 Philip Ardagh
Illustrations © 2017, 2018 Tom Morgan-Jones

A CIP catalogue record for this book is available
from the British Library upon request

ISBN: 978-1-78112-926-5

Printed in China by Leo

In memory of my father,
who used to make
car journeys pass faster
with meandering tales

— PA

In memory of my father, who took me on the best painting
adventures. Some people called him Ants, even though he
wasn't two or more ants, he was 100% human, and I called
him Pop, even though I never once saw him explode

— TMJ

CONTENTS

The First Quest

Norman the Norman from Normandy

The Second Quest

Norman the Norman
and the Very Small Duchess

Chapter 1

Out Come the Swords

Norman the Norman was from Normandy.

Here's Normandy, or a small part of it. With cows.

Here's Norman.

Here's a squirrel eating an acorn (because squirrels are cute).

Norman the Norman from Normandy got up every morning, wearing nothing but his helmet and his chainmail, and ran around his bedroom waving his sword. He was careful not to break anything ... but often not quite careful enough.

CRASH!

See what I mean?

Norman's sword was a great big Norman broad sword. It used to be Great Big Norman's great big Norman broad sword.

Great Big Norman was Norman's father. Like
his sword, he was broad. He would STILL be
Norman's father if he hadn't got into a fight
with ten Bretons from Brittany.

When Great Big Norman first met the Bretons, they all got along fine, laughing and joking and talking about battles they'd been in. Fine, that is, until Great Big Norman trod on one of the Breton's toes. It hurt, but Great Big Norman didn't notice what he'd done, so he didn't say sorry. Then the Bretons made the mistake of TELLING him – not asking him – to apologise.

A fight broke out. Fists flew. Furniture flew. A passing pigeon flew. That squirrel from earlier got flu. And then out came the swords.

The fight didn't last long. Great Big Norman managed to kill seven of the ten Bretons from Brittany, which left three Bretons to chop Great Big Norman into three smaller pieces.

One piece each, which was only fair.

But the Bretons were VERY impressed with how brave Great Big Norman had been and how well he had fought. As a mark of respect, they

each wanted to bury him on their own land. But none of them could agree on who should get his great big body and all the glory.

So what did they do?

You guessed it. They buried the three bits
of Great Big Norman in three different graves,
on their three different bits of land. And when
that was done, they sent Norman his father's
sword and they all signed their names at the
bottom of a WE ARE SORRY FOR YOUR LOSS
tapestry.

Chapter 2

No More Little Norman

When the package arrived in the post, Norman didn't find it too hard to guess what was in it. The great big broad sword shape of the package was a clue. And, after that, everything changed. For starters, no one called him "Little Norman" any more. That's what they had called him when Great Big Norman was still around. Now Great Big Norman was no more.

This was also the day that Norman swore to visit each of his father's three graves to pay his respects.

"Stop swearing, Norman," his mother said.

Norman's mother was still VERY much alive. Her name was Norma the Norman from Normandy. She was a very strong and powerful woman. She bent bent iron bars straight for a living. Her sister Nora bent straight iron bars bent, so they were never out of work. Norman was sad that his dad was dead, but he was also proud that his dad had died fighting. After all, that's how most soldiers want to die.

That, or of old age surrounded by loved ones. Or in the middle of a nice big meal of their favourite food.

Splat. Face first in the gravy.

Norma used to give Norman an egg for breakfast every morning. And every breakfast,

Norman used his father's sword to chop the top off the egg. And every morning he ended up chopping rather a lot of other things too. That's

why most things in the kitchen were either stuck together with glue or tied together with string. And why their servant, Bog, used to crawl around the kitchen on all fours until after 9.00 a.m., just to be on the safe side.

But now Norman was about to leave home.

"Good luck, dear," his mum said. "Be sure to say hello to all three bits of your father from me." She handed Norman a large cloth tied into a bundle.

"What's this?" he asked.

"It's a large cloth tied into a bundle," she said.

"I can see that," Norman said. "But what's it for?"

"It's full of useful things," she said.

Norma the Norman from Normandy
picked up her son (Little) Norman the Norman
from Normandy as if he were as light as
a rice-cake. Then she hugged him almost
as hard as a python squeezing its prey.
"Squeeeeeeeeeeeeeeeeeeee!" she said.

Norman went almost as red as a Coke can,
but he didn't mind because he knew that this
was a loving hug. He kissed his mother on the

cheek. It was a bit like kissing a bag of very
lovable walnuts.

And then Norman jumped up onto Truffle
and was ready to go.

Truffle was a tame wild boar, which meant
that he wasn't really wild any more. He was
more of a not-so-wild boar. But he did have
impressive tusks, was VERY bristly and could
make some seriously impressive grunts and
squeals. Because Norman the Norman from
Normandy was far too small to ride a horse,
or a pony or a donkey, he went about by
not-so-wild boar. Truffle was an uncomfortable
and grunty ride, but Norman loved him.

Chapter 3

Rocks and Buns

Norman looked quite a sight as he left that day on Truffle's back, with the cloth tied into a bundle on HIS back and his father's HUGE sword in his hand.

Off he trotted.

Norman was a familiar sight in the nearby villages. Villagers would greet him with a friendly jeer or throw a rock or two at him. There weren't THAT many good-sized rocks to throw, so sometimes a villager would throw a rock and wait for it to bounce off Norman.

Then they'd run up, snatch the rock and scuttle back far enough to get in another good throw.

To tell the truth, Norman quite enjoyed the attention and the "*clang*" if one of the villagers

scored a bullseye when their rock hit his helmet. The villagers were always VERY careful not to hit Truffle by mistake. Even a not-so-wild boar could get VERY angry if hit by a rock.

Norman the Norman from Normandy hadn't travelled for more than a few hours on his quest when he was hit by a different kind of missile – a very stale bun. The bun was so stale that it was almost as HARD as a rock.

It was thrown by a boy of about Norman's age, but this boy was much taller than him – which wasn't hard. His name was Albert, which he said like "Alber", as if he couldn't be bothered to add the "t" to the end. He was the son of a big local landowner, and his clothes were very fine.

"Hi, Norman!" Albert shouted. "Where are you going?"

"I'm off to visit my father's graves," Norman shouted back. "All three of them."

"To avenge your father's death?" Albert called.

Norman had no idea what "avenge" meant – it means "to get revenge" – but he didn't want to admit that he had no idea, so he shouted, "Maybe!"

"Good luck with that," Albert said. And he laughed.

Chapter 4

Norman the Norman in Brittany

That night, Norman and Truffle slept under the stars. For such a bristly pig, Truffle was

very huggable. Neither pig nor boy was stupid, so they snuggled together to keep each other warm.

It became very cold in the night, and the bundle Norman's mum had given him wasn't big enough to contain a blanket. Or a tent.

The next morning, Norman got up in his chainmail, yawned, stretched, put on his helmet, picked up his father's old sword and swung it about.

It sliced off the branch of a tree just above him, and this landed on his head. If Norman hadn't been wearing his helmet, he'd have knocked himself out cold. As it was, he was now seeing more stars than he'd seen all night.

Truffle was awake too, and he was off snuffling for acorns with that impressive snout of his. Soon both boar and boy were ready to go.

After a few more days and nights, and a few minor adventures – one of which involved a cabbage thief and another a trained jackdaw – Norman the Norman from Normandy arrived in Brittany.

Chapter 5

The First Grave Mistake

The first person Norman went to visit was
Eric the Fearful. He parked Truffle out of sight
around the corner from Eric the Fearful's castle
and gave him a large bag of acorns to chew
while he visited the first of his father's three
graves.

Norman was very aware that he was SO
much smaller than his father. He didn't want
to look even less impressive by turning up on
piggy back.

And so, Norman marched up to the castle gates and banged on them with the handle of his sword. A little door opened and the Captain of the Guard stepped out. "Yes?" he demanded.

"I am here to visit the grave of my father," said Norman.

The Captain of the Guard glared at him as if he were a small piece of very common fly poo. "And who might your father be?"

"Great Big Norman the Norman from Normandy," Norman said. He waved the huge broad sword above his head and almost knocked himself off his feet with the weight of it.

The colour drained from the Captain's face. The truth be told, it drained from all of his body, right the way down to his feet, but – because he was covered in chainmail – only his face showed.

His whole expression changed too. He
was still looking down at Norman, what with
Norman being SO much smaller than him, but

he was no longer looking down ON him. His eyes were now filled with respect.

"Please wait here!" the Captain of the Guard said, and he rushed off to find Eric the Fearful.

Eric rushed down to greet Big Norman the Norman's son. "You're a little smaller than your father," he observed.

"Most people are," Norman said. "He was built like a castle."

"And he was also very brave," said Eric.

"Indeed," Norman said. "But where is your bit of him buried?"

"Over there," said Eric, and he pointed to a rather nice spot under an oak tree behind Norman.

Norman rested his broad sword on his shoulder and turned to take a look. And, as he turned, he accidentally chopped off Eric the Fearful's head. This was unfortunate enough, but even more unfortunate was that he didn't notice what he'd done because his back was turned.

So Norman didn't say "Sorry!" He was already striding over to the grave where his father's legs were buried.

When the Captain of the Guard came out to find Eric the Fearful, he found that his master's head was no longer attached to his master's body. He looked over to Norman, who had finished paying his respects to his father's legs and feet and was now on the move again.

"Like father like son!" the Captain of the Guard muttered under his breath. "Cool as a cucumber!"

The Captain ordered two of his men to carry Eric's body inside, and then he went and got a large dustpan and brush for the head. He used the dustpan with the long, upright handle, to save him from having to bend down. He couldn't wait to tell the other captains of the other guards that his master had had the honour of being killed by Great Big Norman the Norman's son Norman!

Chapter 6

The Second Grave Mistake

Norman was blissfully unaware of what he'd done as he headed off in the direction of the Château of the Duc de Quack.

Duc is French for "Duke", so there was nothing silly about his name at all. So no giggling. "Quack!"

On the way, Norman rescued eleven nuns from a burning nunnery. He rescued two of

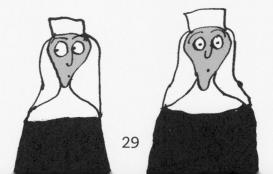

them twice, because they'd gone back in to rescue the nunnery cat, Salmon. Norman ended up having to rescue Salmon too.

Norman also helped a village that was living in fear of a great big snake that simply sat there and stared at them but never did anything. The snake turned out to be an old fire hose that someone had drawn a pair of googly eyes on.

And he saved the life of an enormous toad that was so grateful it decided to hop up on the top of Norman's helmet and enjoy the ride.

When Norman arrived at the Duc's château, Truffle was quite happy to stay out of sight, but the toad insisted on coming in with him. They found the Duc de Quack in the middle of his garden, in the middle of a red rose bush. He was having a fight with the bush because it had been REALLY annoying him. The bush seemed to be winning – the Duc de Quack was surrounded by thorny stems. His Head

Gardener was watching and "tutting" from a safe distance.

"Hello," said Norman. "I'm here to see some of my father."

"Some of him?" the Duc snarled, and he punched a rose so hard that the red petals scattered like a nosebleed.

"He was Great Big Norman of Normandy."

The Duc de Quack stood stock still. Norman's words drifted on a light breeze into the Head Gardener's hairy ears.

"His g-g-grave is over there," said the Duc. "I'll join you just as soon as I've destroyed this bush."

"Let me help!" said Norman, who was a polite young Norman. He slashed at the thorny stems with his sword, then turned before his handiwork was done. So he didn't see that he'd also cut the Duc de Quack in two. But the toad saw and he went "Ribbit!" because he'd spent too much time with frogs.

"Wow!" the Head Gardener said. Then he ordered the Gardener and Under Gardener to get two wheelbarrows – one for the Duc's top half, and one for his bottom half, which included his actual bottom.

After Norman had visited the grave of his father's torso and arms, and muttered a few sad words, such as, "Miss you, Dad," and "Mum says hi," he now headed for the third and final grave.

On the way, Norman pulled a thorn from a lion's paw, stuck a thorn in a different lion's paw – there was a circus in town – and then he rescued a thirsty princess who'd fallen down a well.

Chapter 7

The Third Grave Mistake

The third and final grave was inside a stone casket in the middle of a courtyard in the middle of a castle. This castle's owner, Bernard the Breton, was NOT about to let Norman inside.

That's because news travels fast.

The carrier pigeon who delivered the message that Norman was on his way had stopped for two fingers of KitKat and a cup of sweet tea. But, even so, Bernard knew ALL about how Norman the Norman from Normandy had avenged the death of his father by killing Eric the Fearful and the Duc de Quack. Bernard had instructed Stuart the Steward to instruct all his staff to make sure that NO VISITORS got inside the castle.

"Go away!" Bernard shouted from the highest window in the highest tower when he saw Norman climbing off Truffle's back with the toad on his helmet.

"Hello, Monsieur Bernard!" Norman shouted with a friendly wave or two.

Well, he thought they were friendly waves, but one wave was with the hand Norman was holding his father's broad sword in, so Bernard the Breton thought it was a threatening sword-shake.

"Pleeeeeeease go away!" Bernard shouted. Bernard the Breton was always scared, ever since his wife had vanished after making a rude comment about the local witch's curtains.

The toad, which Norman had named Toad, hopped off Norman's head and managed to find his way into the castle by squeezing through gaps like only toads and frogs and snails and mice – and any other squeeze-through-tiny-spaces animals I've forgotten – can. He hopped up the winding spiral stairs of the highest tower and into the room where Bernard was standing.

Toad hopped up onto the window sill to get eye to eye with Bernard the Breton. Bernard looked at Toad. Toad looked at Bernard and went "Ribbit".

Now – like most people – Bernard the Breton found it hard to tell the difference between frogs and toads, but what he DID know was that frogs, not toads, went "Ribbit".

Bernard ALSO knew that witches and wicked stepmothers and so on often turned princes and princesses into FROGS.

Now, Bernard had never considered his wife to be a princess. She reminded him more of a very cuddly owl. But he loved cuddly owls and he loved his wife. And he missed her. And she had disappeared after she'd upset that witch. Could the witch have turned HER into a frog?

Could this be her? Had she found her way back to him?

There was only one way to find out. He would kiss her. That should work. That's what turned enchanted frogs back into their proper human form.

Far down below, outside the castle, Norman was still waving frantically ... when he saw ... No, it couldn't be? Surely not? That was Toad with Bernard the Breton? It was. It was his new friend Toad!

"Cooooooeeeee!" Norman waved.

At that moment, Bernard's lips touched the top of Toad's head. Unfortunately, Toad was a

very poisonous toad. He was so poisonous that
even people who made poison-tipped darts for
their blowpipes were very polite to him and
would only go near him if they were wearing
three pairs of gloves and were wrapped in a
mattress. In another room.

Bernard the Breton made a noise like a
washing machine stuffed with dirty pants and
toppled out of the highest window in the highest

tower. He left Toad just enough time to hop back onto the sill.

Fortunately, Bernard landed in the back of an empty cart. The fall still killed him, but it made it very easy for Stuart the Steward to wheel his body to the family chapel, and there wasn't nearly so much mess for the servants to clear up.

Stuart ordered the gatekeepers to open the gates and let the son of Great Big Norman the Norman from Normandy in to see his father's grave at once, before he gave anyone else that look …

The steward had assumed that the look he'd seen on Norman's face was a special killer look. In fact, it was one of surprise on spotting Toad. But Stuart the Steward didn't want to be looked at in that way. No, sir. So Norman was welcomed in, and he paid his respects to his father's head. And he told him that Norma the Norman sent her love too.

Norman was delighted by the kind reception he'd had from all three Bretons who'd buried all three bits of his dad. And so he decided to head for home on Truffle with his new friend Toad.

Chapter 8

The Avenger of Death

As he made his way back across Brittany, Norman saved a fish from drowning, helped a chicken cross the road, and showed a peasant farmer how to tie his shoe laces. He'd already done all the big heroic deeds on his way there, so now he was running out of good deeds to do.

When Norman crossed back into Normandy, Truffle had a new spring in his not-so-wild-boar step. Truffle was probably biased, but Normandy acorns tasted SO much better than the Brittany ones! Toad was happy wherever he was, as long as he could spend most of his time sitting on Norman's Norman helmet.

Albert – you remember him, the rich kid who didn't bother to say the "t" at the end of his name – was one of the first people to greet Norman. Instead of throwing a stale bun at him, he gave him a special kind of pastry that Normans get excited about.

"Welcome back!" he cried. "So you DID avenge the death of your father!"

"Did I?" Norman said. He still didn't know what "avenge" meant.

When Norman reached the villages near his home, none of the villagers threw old rocks at him, scurried over, picked them up and threw them again. No, this boy was a hero. He had avenged his father's death AND upheld the honour of Normandy against Brittany. They now had brand NEW rocks to throw, hundreds of them, all the perfect size and in polished wooden buckets. Only the best rocks would do for Norman ...

... but their job was made all the harder now Norman had a toad on his head. Now they had to avoid upsetting the not-so-wild boar AND the poisonous-looking toad.

Chapter 9

Welcome Home, Norman!

When at last Norman reached home, the squirrel had got better from its bout of flu.

If you don't remember the squirrel or the flu, or just the squirrel and not the flu, or just the flu and not the squirrel, then turn back to Chapter 1.

Norma, Norman's mother, was waiting for him. She was picking up bent bars from a pile of bent bars, straightening them and putting them in another pile. Her sister Nora was then taking them, bending them and putting them back in the first pile.

"You're home!" Norma cried, and she kissed her boy on the top of his head. Or where the top of his head would be if he weren't wearing a helmet. With a toad on top. So in fact Norma kissed Toad instead ...

... which wasn't a problem. This is Norma we're talking about. Norma the Norman from Normandy. Hers is one tough family. Don't believe me? You should meet her son, Norman. He's a hero and a fighter like his dad.

The only thing is, he doesn't know it.

An Afterword

Are you wondering what was in the large
cloth tied into a bundle that Norman's mother,
Norma, gave Norman before he set off on his
travels? It was a slightly smaller cloth, in case
he lost the first one. And you can guess what
was inside that.

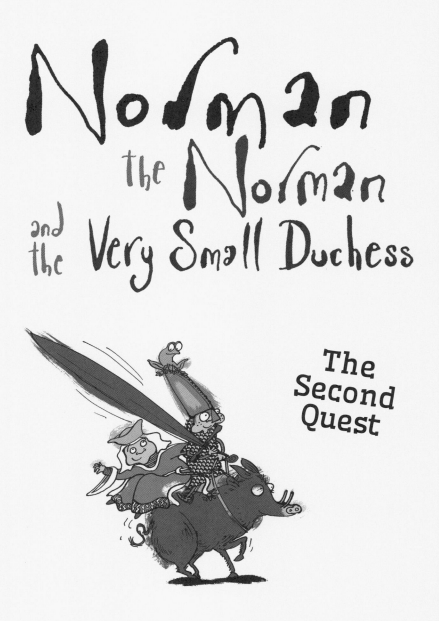

Norman the Norman and the Very Small Duchess

The Second Quest

Chapter 1
The Future Past

Norman the Norman from Normandy woke up with a big yawn and rolled over.

He kept rolling over and over and over and over. You get the picture. And if you don't get the picture, here's a picture.

See? A LOT of rolling over. And eyes wide open in surprise.

The reason WHY Norman the Norman from Normandy was so surprised was because when he normally rolled out of bed, he normally hit his bedroom floor with a THUMP. And that was an end to it. So, this time around – and around and around – he didn't know why he was STILL rolling. And rolling.

Then he remembered. He hadn't gone to sleep in his bed the night before. He'd gone to sleep at the top of the hill.

If you're thinking "WHY didn't he go to sleep in his bed?", that's a very good question. Which is why I am going to answer it.

Chapter 2
Conquest!

Meet William, Duke of Normandy.

He was in charge of Normandy. Normandy was his dukedom, which is why he was called a duke. Or maybe Normandy was called his dukedom BECAUSE he was a duke. Either way, William, Duke of Normandy, was very proud of his Norman nose.

One day, the Duke was sitting in his castle when his wife came into the room. She was small. Very small. She was the kind of person who was so small that even small people called her small.

Even mice pointed and laughed at her. Look. Here's one and that's EXACTLY what it's doing.

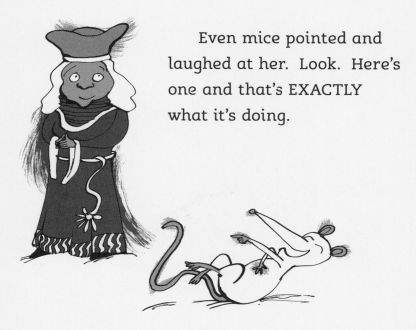

"Hello, Mat," the Duke said. His wife's name was Matilda, but he called her "Mat" for short because everything ABOUT her was short.

"Hello," Matilda said. "Have you heard about Norman?"

"Is that the boy who saved a cart full of nuns from sinking in a stinking swamp, then saved the swamp from developers, then saved the developers from an angry dragon by telling the dragon that dragons don't exist?"

"Yes, that's the one," Matilda said with a nod.

"Then yes," said the Duke. "I have heard of him."

And yes, dear reader, that's the same Norman the Norman who goes rolling down that hill. Only it HASN'T HAPPENED YET. We've gone back to BEFORE the hill-rolling happened to find out how it came to pass.

"I think he should come on your conquest thingy with you," said Matilda.

In truth, William, Duke of Normandy, got cross when his wife called his plans for the Conquest of England his "conquest thingy". He wanted his conquest to be big and brave and grand and CONQUESTY.

"Conquest thingy" made it sound like something you might stop off to do on the way to the shops, if you remember and have the time. William's plan was to sail over to England, conquer it and become KING.

But William did like Matilda's idea of asking Norman along.

"I need the very best Normans at my side when we conquer England, and there are many tales told about young Norman and his bravery," he said. "I'll order him to come to my castle right now."

Chapter 3
Captured!

There was a knock at Norman the Norman from Normandy's front door. It was Barry, the Duke's messenger. Barry was a bit nervous about knocking. He had heard stories about the tiny young Norman who didn't know the meaning of the word "fear".

Tales of Norman's bravery – and tales of how he didn't know the meaning of some words – were told around the fire. And if people were too poor to afford firewood or, at the very least, a box of matches, then they would tell tales around their PRETEND fire, or where their fire would be if they had one.

Barry, the Duke's messenger, knocked again.
Harder this time.

Norman was busy trying to put up a picture.
The first thing was to hammer a nail into the
wall with the hilt – handle – of his sword.

No. That's not true.

The first thing Norman had to do was to stand on Truffle's back, to reach the spot where he had to hammer in the nail. Truffle was Norman's not-so-wild boar. Norman rode him instead of a horse. And he used him instead of a ladder for small jobs around the house. Norman was up on Truffle's back when Barry did the second, louder, knock.

Truffle was in a daydream about acorns. He jumped in surprise and charged. He banged through the front door, without opening it, as Norman held on tight.

Barry was startled. He threw himself to the side to be safe. He fell to the dusty ground with a THUNK! A shower of great big splinters of front door fell down on top of him.

"Sorry!" Norman shouted, at the very moment that Truffle decided to stop in his

tracks. But Norman kept on going. He flew
through the air and landed in a bush.

"Ooof!"

There was a cry of pain, and it wasn't from
Norman. Norman looked down and saw that
he'd landed on someone. What he didn't know
was that this was a robber. The robber had
been following Barry, the Duke's messenger, for
the last three miles. The robber rolled out into
the open with Norman on top of him. Norman
still had his sword in his hand.

"I s-surrender!" the robber said.

"Oh," Norman said. "Good ... I think."

Barry the messenger was stunned. Norman
must have spotted the robber and grabbed his
sword off him before the front door had even
opened! All the stories about Norman the
Norman from Normandy were true!

"Here," the robber said as he sat up. "Are
you Great Big Norman's boy, Norman?"

Norman nodded. His helmet tilted forward
and covered his eyes. "I am," he said.

"Then it's a great honour to be captured by you," the robber said. "Have a croissant." He reached inside his tunic, pulled out a croissant and handed it to Norman, who was still sitting on him. It was only a bit squashed (a bit like the robber himself).

"Thank you," Norman said.

"It's still fresh," the robber said. "I stole it this morning."

Barry was up on his feet again. He dusted himself down. "I'm sorry to bother you," he said as he walked over to the mighty Norman. All of a sudden, he was worried that Norman might not WANT to come to the Duke's castle. And what could he do then? "William, your Duke, told me to ask you to come to his castle at once," he told Norman.

Norman climbed off the robber. "Really?" he said. "I like castles. Does it have a moat?"

"Well, it has a ditch all the way round it," said Barry. "A very deep ditch."

"But that's not quite the same as a moat, is it?" Norman said. "What about a gift shop?"

Barry thought hard. "Well, the Duke does sometimes give people nice presents."

Norman still wasn't sure. "Does it have a tea room?" he asked.

Barry thought of the Duke of Normandy's enormous banqueting hall. Perfect for enormous banquets. "Yes," he said. "A really good one."

"My mum and I do like a castle with a good tea room," Norman said. "I'll come."

Chapter 4

What a Welcome!

Norman the Norman rode into the courtyard of the Duke's castle. There was Duchess Matilda, ready to greet him. The first thing he saw was that she was a sensible size. She was about the same size as him.

On the way to William's castle, he and Barry had stopped so that Truffle could have a drink of water. But then Norman had tripped over the end of his belt, which was hanging down, and he'd fallen forward.

Somehow his Norman broad sword ended up stuck in the chest of Normandy's last remaining giant.

The giant had been hiding between two very big trees at the side of the road. (He was pretending to be a third very big tree.)

The last remaining giant – who was no longer remaining – fell to the ground as lifeless as a very big sack of dead rocks.

"Blimey!" Barry said, which is Norman for "God blind me!" (Or, if it isn't, it should be.)

A crowd of people from the village came to see the dead giant and cheered. He'd been bothering them for months – he'd stolen their food, sat on their houses and drunk all the water from their ponds.

One family took the shirt off the giant's body and then made it into eleven pairs of curtains, a sail for a boat, a tent, some dish cloths and – er – a much smaller shirt.

But this didn't all happen at once. They were still busy trying to pull the shirt off the dead giant as Norman the Norman and Barry left.

The first thing the Duchess Matilda spotted when she first laid eyes on Norman was that Norman was every bit as small as she hoped he would be. She marched across the cobbles of the castle courtyard and looked him in the eye. She didn't even have to climb on a pile of egg boxes to do it.

Their eyes were the same distance from the ground. Matilda gave an excited squeal and did an excited little jump up into the air. (She could only do little jumps.)

The jump gave her lady-in-waiting, Lady Marie, a bit of a shock. It was Lady Marie's job to follow Matilda around everywhere and to wait – she was the lady-in-waiting, after all.

Lady Marie wasn't sure what she was waiting for. So she kept on waiting, to find out.

"Welcome!" Matilda said, and she threw her
arms wide.

Norman the Norman wasn't sure what the correct way to greet the Duchess was, so he copied what she did – he threw HIS arms wide too.

Yes, of course he was holding his dad's great big heavy sword. The sword cut the bottom of a wooden dovecote in half. The dovecote fell to the ground – and it only just missed Norman's friend and pet toad, Toad – and then startled white doves came flapping out.

The doves all perched on the nearest thing, which was Norman the Norman from Normandy with his arms out wide. He looked like a cross made of white doves.

If there isn't a picture of this here, there should be.

Thank you. And what a splendid picture it is too.

Matilda had never seen anything like it. It was like the best greeting EVER.

"It tickles," Norman said.

But, because his mouth was full of white feathers, no one could understand what he was saying.

Chapter 5
Nosh

A banquet had been prepared in Norman's honour. A pile of books was put on Norman's chair so that he could see over the top of the banqueting table. Back then, books were written by hand, bound in leather and cost a LOT of money. So it was very special for Norman to be allowed to park his bottom on top of them. Normally, only the Duchess was allowed to sit on books.

Servants were busy putting pewter platters piled high with mouth-watering goodies on the table. There were no knives and forks because

no one had got around to inventing forks yet.
They didn't have the tine.*

*This is a fork joke which only works if:

a) you know that the right word for the prong
of a fork is a *tine*,

and

b) you think waste of *tine* sounds a bit like
waste of *time*.

And they didn't put knives on the table because
everyone used their own dagger.

William, Duke of Normandy, had just made
a nice speech to welcome Norman and say how
proud he was that Norman would be part of the
Norman invasion going over to England to claim
the English crown.

Of course, Norman was only half-listening. (He was feeding titbits to Truffle, who was lying next to his chair like a dog with big tusks.)

Norman thought that the crown was just that – a crown that went on someone's head. He thought that claiming the crown would be like going into his local baker's shop and claiming a free croissant.

Norman didn't understand that William meant that he was going to fight to become KING OF ENGLAND. And that Norman would be one of the soldiers to fight with him.

When they'd all sat down to eat the feast, Norman remembered that he didn't have a dagger of his own. He looked around.

"Please," the man next to him said. He was Odo, Bishop of Bayeux (which rhymes with mayo, which is short for a sort of fancy salad cream). "Use one of my daggers. I always carry a spare." He leaned forward and pulled a dagger from his boot. He wiped it on his sleeve and handed it to Norman.

"No need, thank you," Norman said. He took out his broad sword, but he couldn't balance it. The broad sword swished across the table, towards the Duke.

Everyone in eye-shot looked on in HORROR.

Chapter 6

Ooops!

Once in a while, people tried to kill William. Not simply because he was William but because he was the Duke of Normandy and they wanted his job. It was the top job in Normandy. No one could tell you what to do.

Anyone who tried to kill William ended up:

- being given a stern telling-off
- tortured
- then executed.

It was lucky for the Duke AND for Norman that Norman's Norman broad sword missed William.

A servant was about to pour a drink from
a large jug into William's goblet. The tip of the
sword hit the jug instead.

The jug smashed into 22 bits. Drink went everywhere. Duke William jumped to his feet. He didn't want to get soaked, and he didn't like the look of THE BIG BROADSWORD.

Toad sat in the middle of the table. He was soaking wet. He gave a massive burp for a toad (which was still a big burp for a human).

BURP!

Matilda jumped to her feet. This made her look even smaller, because she was taller when she was sitting on HER pile of books on

HER chair. She clapped her hands in delight. "Norman just saved your life, William!" she yelped.

Have I? Norman thought.

"How so?" the Duke asked.

"Didn't you see?" Matilda said. "That toad was in the jug. One of the most poisonous kinds of toad there is! So poisonous that it will have poisoned the drink! The very drink you were about to drink!"

William, Duke of Normandy, peered at Toad. "Are you sure it's not a frog?"

"Ribbet," Toad said. He used to spend a lot of time with frogs.

"See?" the Duke said. "That's a frog! Frogs say 'Ribbet'!"

Oh, there you are, Toad, Norman thought. *I didn't know where you'd hopped off to.*

Matilda pulled the top book off the stack of books on her chair. "Look!" she said, and pointed. The book was called MY FIRST BIG BOOK OF TOADS.

The tiny duchess used both hands to open the huge leather book.

Inside, the book was beautiful. Everything was written in hand in Latin by someone who was very good with a pen. Some of the bigger letters had little pictures drawn inside them in bright colours, including gold. And some of the pages were taken up with one big picture of one big toad. The Duchess Matilda flipped through the pages until she came to one picture which looked a LOT like Toad.

"There!" Matilda said, and she pointed in triumph.

Toad tilted his head to admire the picture this way, then that. If he'd had a pen with him, I think he might have signed it with his name.

The Duke came around the table, bent down and threw his arms around Norman the Norman. "You saved my life!" he said. "Thank you!"

"My pleasure," Norman said. He didn't tell William that Toad was HIS toad. Why bother such an important man with such an unimportant detail?

Toad jumped up onto Norman's helmet.

"Ribbet," he said. It was the only noise Toad ever made, apart from burps.

Chapter 7

All the Latest News

A very small, very old lady scuttled out from under the banqueting table and started to sew very fast indeed.

She looked up at Norman. "How do?" she said, and rubbed her nose on her sleeve.

"H-Hello," Norman said. He turned to Bishop Odo and asked in a soft voice, "Who's she?"

"She's Gran," Odo said. "She works for me. As well as being Bishop of Bayeux, I run a local news-tapestry."

"What's a news-tapestry?" asked Norman.

"It's an embroidery that reports all the local news in pictures," the bishop explained.

"If it's an embroidery, why do you call it a news-tapestry and not a news-embroidery?" Norman asked.

"Because a news-tapestry sounds more high-tech," Bishop Odo explained. "Tapestries are made with LOOMS, and a loom is a machine. People love machines! It sounds much more

exciting than a room full of old ladies doing
embroidery with their needles."

"Oh," said Norman.

"Ribbet," said Toad on his helmet.

Odo looked at Toad nervously. "I think he likes you," he said.

"And I like him," said Norman.

"Good," Odo said, and he told Norman more about the news-tapestry. "I have people called news-recorders whose job it is to embroider all the latest news. Gran here is one of them. She's live at the scene, reporting on your arrival at the castle. Look."

He held up one end of the embroidery that the little old lady was working on. It was beautiful – a picture in embroidery of Norman smashing the jug. The Duke looked startled and Toad was jumping out.

"Wow," Norman said. "That IS good. And she's your gran?"

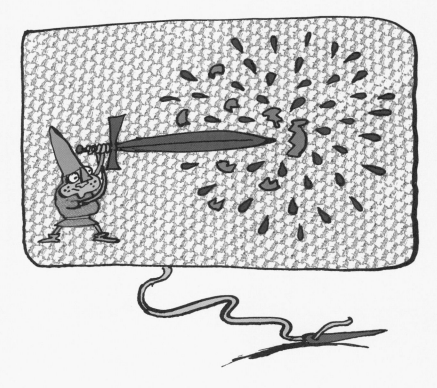

"No, no, no," Odo said. "Gran is her name. I
think it's short for Grandmother. I'm William's
half-brother," he went on. "I'll fight with
William when he conquers England, but because
I'm a bishop, it would be wrong if I had a sword."

"I see." Norman nodded. Toad nodded
too. He had to nod whether he liked it or not,
because he was sitting on Norman's helmet.

"I can't have a sword," said Odo. "So I use a club. A really BIG club. Gran will come with us to England," he went on. "She will record our victory over the English."

"Victory? Are we going to win, then?" Norman asked as he bit into something that had been put in front of him. It was a pewter plate and it hurt his teeth.

Bishop Odo gave him a look. "Well, we're not going all the way over there to lose, are we?"

"Great," said Norman.

Chapter 8

The Selfie Embroidery

After the banquet, the Duchess Matilda stood next to Norman in front of the best mirror in the palace. They looked at themselves in the mirror, and Duchess Matilda did a quick embroidery that showed her and Norman standing side by side.

"What are you doing, lady duke person?" Norman asked. He tried to sound as polite as possible.

"It's called a selfie," Matilda told him. "You are a great ambassador for little people, Norman. You show that heroes come in ALL shapes and sizes."

Toad jumped back up onto Norman's
helmet. (He had been too shy to be in the selfie
embroidery.)

"No more chit-chat!" Duke William said with
a smile. He walked across the stone floor and
gave Norman a friendly slap on the back.

The slap on the back was so hard it made
Norman lurch forward. He missed the mirror

and bumped into a tapestry hanging on the wall. There was a spy hiding behind it, who now toppled out of a window with a cry.

This cry, in fact:

"Arrrrrrrrrrrrrrrrrrrrrrrrrrrrrrrrrrrrrrrr-rrrrrrrrrrrgh!"

The spy would have landed in the moat with a loud SPLASH if there had been a moat. As it was, he landed in the ditch with a less cheery CRUNCH.

A group of soldiers peered out of the window at the same time as another lot ran downstairs to find out who the spy was and what he'd been up to.

"You're a one-man army!" the Duke said. He turned back to Norman and gave him a hug. "You keep saving my life! Tomorrow, we sail for England and I want you by my side."

Chapter 9

On a Roll

And so the Duke and his army made their way to the seaside, where the ships waited for them on the beach.

"Tomorrow the conquest begins!" he said. "Tonight we set up camp!"

William was a duke, so he didn't have to do any setting up of the camp himself. He had a whole ARMY to do that for him. While that was going on, Norman and Truffle went for a walk. Truffle found a rather fine stash of acorns, so by the time they got back, most of the others had gone to bed. And Norman didn't know which was HIS tent, so Norman and Truffle decided to sleep side by side under the stars.

In the night, Norman rolled over in his sleep and kept on rolling. He opened his eyes in surprise. Yes, it was THAT rolling over. The one at the beginning of this story. When Norman got to the bottom, the rolling stopped and he sat up. Toad hopped back up onto his helmet. Truffle bounded down the hill after them. This was out of loyalty and love, and also because he knew Norman had some of those fine acorns left in his pocket.

"Well," said Norman as he got up onto the not-so-wild boar, "we may as well go home now."

He arrived at his house just as his mother, Norma the Norman from Normandy, was out front.

Norma was a very strong woman. Her job was to bend bent iron bars straight. She was getting ready for her day when she saw Norman. "Hello, son," she said as she gave Norman a hug. "Where have you been?"

"I went to look around a castle," Norman said.

"Did it have a moat?" she asked.

Norman shook his head. "No, but it did have a big ditch all the way round."

"That's not quite the same," Norma said. "What about a gift shop?"

Norman shook his head again. "No. But it had a nice tea room. More of a banqueting hall, I suppose."

"Lovely," Norma said. "You're just in time for breakfast. Your egg should be ready."

"Thanks, Mum," said Norman, and he walked into his house and straight to the kitchen with a slight limp. (The limp was because of that mother/son hug he'd just had.)

Norman lifted his Norman broad sword, ready to cut the top off his egg.

Norma smiled at the loud CRASHES and
BANGS, and at the cry of their servant as he
ducked for cover.

It was good to have Norman home.

An Afterword

Bishop Odo went on to produce a special edition of the Bayeux Tapestry – which was really an embroidery. It was all about William's victory in England (where he became king). Matilda became England's smallest ever queen (so far). Bishop Odo used English embroiderers to sew the so-called tapestry because they were cheaper. And, of course, Norman, Truffle and Toad aren't in the Bayeux Tapestry because they missed the boat. But Odo is. With his great big bishop's club.

Some TRUE and INTERESTING things about the NORMANS and NORMANDY

I hope you've had fun reading about Norman the Norman from Normandy. I've had fun writing about him, and about Truffle too! The BIG question about this little Norman is did he really exist? Well, YOU can decide that. But what *is* true is the history behind Norman's silly adventures.

When some (very sensible) people think of the Normans, they think of cheese. There are LOTS of different types of cheese made in the part of France called Normandy. They are all DELICIOUS. (I tested them, so you don't have

to.) A selection of cheeses is called "a smell".*
(*Actually, I just made that last bit up.)

But when MOST people think of
the Normans, they think of castles
and Norman soldiers, chainmail and
helmets with funny nose-guards, just like
you see Norman wearing in the story. And,
of course, the most famous Norman soldier of
all was William the Conqueror, who invaded
England in 1066 in the Norman Conquest.

William needed lots of brave soldiers to fight
for him, and some of them were as fearsome
as Norman's dad, Big Norman. They landed on
a beach near the town of Pevensey in England,
and the Battle of Hastings really DID take
place – not in Hastings but in a field nearby.
There's a town called Battle there now (which is
where my mother lives).

The Norman soldiers used broad swords just
like the one Norman the Norman waved about.
This powerful weapon had a blade on both

edges, so it was good for cutting and slashing people. It was heavy – around 1.25kg (about three bags of sugar) – and was 76cm long with a pointy end that could be used to stick into someone. Ouch!

As for Matilda, Duchess of Normandy and later Queen of England, she really was tiny. She was also far more posh than William. Her grandfather and her uncle were kings of France, while William's parents, Robert, Duke of Normandy, and a woman called Herleva, weren't even married. This was a big deal back then. And then there was the fact that Herleva's dad – William's grandfather – was a tanner who made leather from animal hides, dyeing them with – er – people's poo, which was all a bit embarrassing. William was teased about this a lot, even when he was grown up, but people teased him less when he became a king with a BIG ARMY.

William really did have a half-brother called Odo, by the way, and he really WAS the Bishop of Bayeux and in charge of the tapestry.

In truth, very brainy historians – with huge heads to fit those big brains inside them – think that the Bayeux Tapestry was probably made by English women in England … and AFTER the battle, not during it. But it really was embroidered, which means sewn by hand, rather than being a true tapestry, which would have been woven on a loom. It was then taken to Normandy and hung in Bayeux Cathedral.

William, Duke of Normandy, *also known as* William the Conqueror, *also known as* William I of England, became king in 1066. In 1085 he ordered a survey of all of England, which meant that an enormous list was made of all the buildings, lands and people. This information was recorded in the Domesday Book, which, just to confuse matters, was actually TWO books. Amazingly it still exists over 900 years later, and the final version was written up by one person. And why did William want all this information? So he knew what was in the land that he had just conquered. Then he could get the English to pay him money because he was their new king. That's called TAX, and William always wanted to make more MONEY, of course. That's what kings did.

Once William had invaded England and taken all the land and titles to give to his

faithful Norman followers, lots of Norman (old French) words crept into the English language. They didn't replace the Anglo-Saxon words that went before them, though. Instead, they existed alongside each other. As a result, English often has more than one word for the same thing. For example, there is both the Anglo-Saxon word "ghost" and the old French word "phantom", as well as "weep" and "cry", and "forgive" and "pardon", and "weird" and "strange", and many, many more!

Like Big Norman, William the Conqueror's death was far less glorious than his victory at (near) Hastings. He was injured when he was trying to capture the French town of Mantes and taken back to the Norman capital of Rouen. He knew he was going to die, so he gave his treasures to the poor and to the Church. He even went so far as to send gifts to Mantes for them to rebuild some of their churches, which he had – er – burned when trying to seize the town! He wanted God to forgive him.

When William did die, the rich Normans who'd been at his bedside rushed off to their homes and lands to look after them (because they didn't know who might take over from him), and the less rich "seized the arms, vessels, clothing, linen, and all the royal furnishings, and hurried away leaving the king's body almost naked on the floor of the house".

And if you think THAT was bad, wait until we get to what happened to William's body next. William was going to be buried in the Abbaye-aux-Hommes at Caen, and his coffin was taken there by boat along the river. But just as the Abbot and the monks were going to bury William, a fire broke out in Caen, and most people had to rush off to try to put it out.

After the funeral, the dead king's body was lowered into the stone sarcophagus (another coffin) he was to be buried in. But the sarcophagus was too small, and when the monks tried to push the body in, it exploded, releasing a terrible smell.

After that, William's son had a fine tomb made for his father's body. In 1562 this was attacked by a mob. They took out William's bones and scattered them all over the place. All that was left was one thigh bone. This was finally buried in 1642, but then it was destroyed in the eighteenth century, during the French Revolution (when the French got rid of their king and royal family). Poor William. Not much rest in peace there.

The English were part of the Allied army that invaded Normandy in 1944, some 878 years after the Normans invaded England. These were the D-Day Landings, and the Allies were fighting the Nazis who had taken over France during the

Second World War, so the Normans welcomed the English and their Allies as friends and liberators.

Things have come a long way since Norman the Norman rode into town on Truffle.

PHILIP ARDAGH
Saint-Agnan-sur-Sarthe,
Normandy, France